I AM CON...

Written By Connor Rodriguez & his Dad

Illustrated By Anju Chaudhary

ISBN 9781654299248

In 2010, we became parents to a very special little boy when our son Connor was born with Down Syndrome*

We dedicate this book to Connor. He has shown us the true beauty of life, and we love him beyond measure! 🖤

You can read more about Connor's journey and about Down Syndrome online at our website; www.connorsplace.org

*Down Syndrome is a genetic disorder caused by trisomy 21 – when there are three rather than two number 21 chromosomes present in every cell of the body.

Hi, my name is Connor, and I'm nine years old. I have a dog named Max and he is my best friend. Some people may say I am different because of the way I look and sound, but I say we are more alike than you think.

Let's take a look and see.

I like to play with my friends. Every day I go to school on the bus, and I am happy to see them. We learn many new things, and at recess, I am excited to play with my friends again.

Do you like to play with your friends?

In school, I learn math, science, reading, and many other subjects. I love to read books, and my favorite book is about a dog named Max.

What type of books do you like to read?

My hair is brown, and I have brown eyes too.
I have friends with brown eyes, blue eyes,
and green eyes.

What color are your eyes?

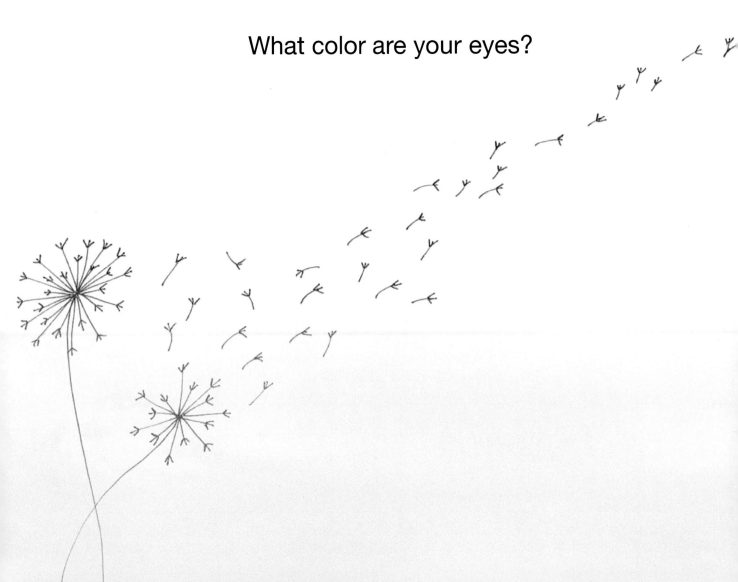

I love to eat fruit like strawberries, blueberries, apples, and bananas. I also love ice cream! Sometimes on the weekends, my dad makes my favorite pancakes with strawberries and bananas for breakfast.

What are your favorite foods?

I like to play all kinds of games like basketball, catch with my dad and soccer, but most of all, I like to play tag.

What is your favorite game?

The colors of the rainbow are so beautiful! I like blue, yellow, red, and orange but my favorite color is purple.

What is your favorite color?

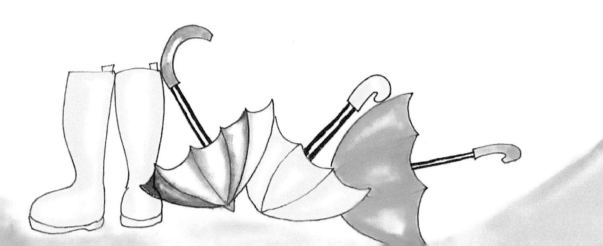

I like to sing and play musical instruments like the drums, guitar, or even a harmonica, but I like to play the piano the most.

What is your favorite musical instrument?

I have traveled to many places like Florida, Pennsylvania, Massachusetts, Greece, and Puerto Rico, but my favorite place is Ireland, where I visit my cousins.

Where is your favorite place to travel?

In the summer I like to go to the beach. Mommy and Daddy help me build sandcastles and dig big holes as if we are digging for buried treasure!

What do you like to do at the beach?

I don't like to get upset. Sometimes when I get upset, I stomp my foot and yell. Sometimes I even cry. But after a little while, I feel better, especially when I see my dog, Max!

What do you do when you get upset?

I like to be happy, and I like my friends and family to be happy too. My favorite question is, "Are you happy?" and my favorite saying is "I love you".

What is your favorite question or saying?

I love to dance and sing, and when the music starts, there is no stopping me!

Do you like to dance and sing?

So, I may sound different and look different, but this is me. My name is Connor. Yes, we are all different, and yet we are all the same!

THE
END

Made in the USA
Coppell, TX
22 February 2020